This book belongs to

_____

_____

To Geraldine for your love and support
M.M.

Published by Albury Books in 2016
Albury Court, Albury, Thame, OX9 2LP, United Kingdom

Sales and Enquiries:
Kuperard Publishers and Distributors
59 Hutton Grove, London, N12 8DS
Tel: +44 (0) 208 446 2440 | Fax: +44 (0) 208 446 2441
sales@kuperard.co.uk | www.kuperard.co.uk

ISBN 978-1-910571-51-4 (paperback)

A CIP catalogue record for this book is available from the British Library
10 9 8 7 6 5 4 3
Printed in the United Kingdom

Imagine Me A Pirate!

Mark Marshall

Albury Children's

I'm lively, fearless and clever,
And as brave as a dog can be!
Always looking for adventure –
So come on a journey with me...

Imagine I'm a pirate,

Upon the open seas.

Sailing in my shipshape boat,

To anywhere I please.

I'd search for buried treasure,
Dig my fortune from the ground,

Silver, gold and diamonds -
All waiting to be found!

Imagine I'm an astronaut,
Blasting into space.

I'd wave to my friends on the Earth below,
And disappear without a trace!

I'd wear a special spacedog's suit
With a helmet for my face.
I could leave my paw prints on the moon,
And offer aliens a race!

Imagine I'm a diver,
Who's made friends with a big blue whale!

He could squirt me with
his water-spout
And catch me with his tail.

Imagine I'm the pilot
Of my own hot air balloon.
I'd spot a stripy zebra
Or catch sight of a baboon!

Imagine I'm an explorer,
Trekking to the cold North Pole.

Fighting the windy weather,
To reach my final goal.

I might just find an igloo
Made from bricks of ice.
And I could join the bear in there –
Now wouldn't that be nice!

I love to dream my doggy dreams –
They challenge and inspire!
But the best place on earth for me right now .
Is curled up and warm
by the fire.

Other **Mark Marshall** books for you to enjoy

Little Lion Lost!
Where has Little Lion's mum gone? Are those her footprints? Follow this brave little cub through the jungle and a series of exciting encounters!

Little Leopard on the Move
Little Leopard will miss his friends when he moves with Mum to their new home. 'Why don't you live with us?' suggest his friends. But will their homes be suitable for a little leopard on the move?!

Little Tiger's Big Holiday
What should Little Tiger pack for his holiday?
He might fly a plane – he'll need some goggles. Or explore the ocean – he'll need a snorkel. But will it all fit in his case?!